Life of Saint Columba / Apostle of Scotland

F. A. Forbes

Chapter I

CHILD OF THE MOUNTAIN AND THE LAKE

FOURTEEN hundred years ago, in the sweet days of autumn, when the woods of Gartan are clothed in crimson and gold, and the still waters of Lough Veagh reflect the deep blue of the skies above, Eithne, the wife of Fedhlimidh, Prince of Tir-Connell, had a strange dream. It seemed to her that an angel of God stood beside her, bearing in his hands a veil scattered all over with the Bowers of Paradise, and that, spreading it out, he bade her admire its beauty. Eithne was a daughter of kings, but never before had she seen so marvellously fair a web; she stretched out her hands to grasp it, but even as she touched it, it rose and fluttered lightly into the air. Over hill, mountain, and lough floated its shadowy loveliness, till it rested at last on the moors and mountains of a land that lay far away in the moaning seas. Then Eithne wept for the loss of the beautiful veil, but the angel comforted her.

"It is but a symbol," he said, "of the son that shall be born to thee in the days to come. He shall be a prince and a prophet; the world shall be perfumed by his holiness; and he shall bear the flower of the faith among the heathen far over land and sea."

When morning came Eithne told her husband of the dream, and the two took counsel together. That his son should be a great prince in no way surprised Fedhlimidh. Was not he himself a grandson of the great king Niall of the Nine Hostages, so called because he had subdued nine Kings of Ireland to his will and made them his vassals, and was not the reigning king of all Ireland his near kinsman? No strange thing would it have been in those turbulent days, when the lives of kings were short and uncertain, were the son of Fedhlimidh himself to be set on the throne as High King of Ireland.

But Eithne's dream seemed to point more to a heavenly supremacy than an earthly; was it an indication of God's will that they should dedicate their child to Him? They thought it was, and a few months later, when heaven sent them a fair and beautiful little son, they earnestly prayed to the Giver of all good gifts that He would take the child, if it seemed well to Him, for His service.

At Teampall-Douglas, a few miles from Gartan, there lived a holy old priest called Cruithnechan; to him they took the babe that it might receive at his hands the holy rites of Baptism. He was given the name of Columba, a not uncommon name in Ireland at the time, and while yet a little child was sent back to the saintly Cruithnechan that the old man might train him in the ways of wisdom and holiness.

In this Columba's parents but followed the custom of the time, for it was usual for the sons of chiefs to be brought up from their earliest youth by some great bard, soldier, or priest, according to their destination in life; and it was the duty of these foster parents to train their charges in all that had to do with their future profession.

The little Columba was an apt pupil. It was his delight to accompany his master to the Church, there to listen to the chanting of the Divine Office; and so keen of ear and quick of memory was the boy that he had learnt some of the psalms by heart before he could spell them out in the Psalter—the lesson-book of every young reader of his time. Cruithnechan himself was unaware of this until one day when he took the child with him on a visit to a brother priest near Derry. The two clerics went together to the Church to chant the Divine Office, and Columba, as was his wont, knelt to pray before the altar.

Now it came to pass that Cruithnechan lost his place, and was in great distress because he could not find it again. The office came to a standstill, and the pause would have been a long one had not the boy's clear treble voice taken up the psalm Where the old man had halted, and chanted sweetly the alternate verses until the missing place was found. It was Columba's love of the Church that won for him among his companions the name by which he became famous in after-days— "Columb-cille" or "the dove of the Church." He would slip away from their games whenever he could, but they always knew where to find him. "He nestles beside the altar like a dove in its nest," they would say.

In spite of the boy's name, however, underneath the strong faith and love, the true and deep devotion that were always his chief characteristics, lay a nature that was in no wise dovelike. Loyal, great-hearted, and compassionate as he undoubtedly was, the blood of the fierce and haughty

Hy-Nialls flowed in his veins. To be quick to take offence and slow to forgive an injury is a characteristic of the Celtic race all the world over, and Columba was no exception to the rule. Long and sharp was to be the struggle before that quick and imperious nature was wholly conquered by the grace of God, but great was to be the victory at last.

To Cruithnechan it was evident that the blessing of God rested in no small degree on the child of his fostering. Returning home one night he saw his house lit up as it were with a great fire, and fearing for the safety of his little charge he entered in haste. All was in darkness within, save over the head of the sleeping child, where there hung a globe of fire. The old man fell on his knees, not knowing what the portent might mean; but God reassured him, showing that the light of His Holy Spirit had been poured out abundantly upon Columba, who was to labour fruitfully in His service.

It has always been acknowledged by the Celtic races that among the children of men there are a chosen few who are gifted with the second sight. Strange instances are given of mortal eyes that have seen the invisible, and of men and women who have known things that are not to be discerned by the senses. A little corner of the veil that hides the spiritual world from the world of sense has been lifted. From the earliest ages, to those who are exceptionally pure of heart and holy, this contact with the spiritual world has been given in a supernatural degree. The materialist may scoff, but the voice of the Ages is louder and clearer in our ears than his.

From his childhood Columba seems to have possessed this gift in a very marked manner. His guardian angel, we are told by his biographers, appeared to him frequently, and the child would talk to him familiarly, and ask him if all the spirits in heaven were as radiant and beautiful as he. One day the angel bade the boy tell him what he would choose if any virtue might be his for the asking.

"I would choose purity and wisdom," answered he.

"Well hast thou chosen, Columba," said the angel, "they shall be thine, and God will add to them yet another gift."

So it came to pass in the course of time that there appeared one day before Columba three beautiful maidens, who would have embraced him, but he pushed them roughly away.

"Dost thou not know us, Columba?" asked one of them, and a celestial radiance shone from her face and garments as she spoke. "We are three sisters sent to thee from our Father, that we may abide with thee for ever."

"I know you not," said Columba. "Who is your father?"

"Our Father is God, the Lord and Saviour of the world," answered the maiden, and her voice was like the music of heaven.

"Truly a noble parentage," said the boy. "By what names do men call you?"

"Our names are Purity, Prophecy, and Wisdom," she answered, "and we have come never to leave thee more, and to love thee with an incorruptible love."

So among the peaceful hills and lakes of Donegal the boy Columba grew into manhood. Tall and fair and straight of limb was the son of Eithne and Fedhlimidh, with a voice clear and sweet as a trumpet-call, and a heart that was fearless, pure, and true. Cruithnechan had done his work well; he had taught Columba all that he knew of earthly lore and of heavenly; but the time of his fostering was over. He must go forth now into the great world that lay beyond the quiet mountains, the world of strife and of tragedy, of joy and of sorrow.

A strange world and one of many contrasts, that of Ireland in the sixth century. To the unanimous voice of Christianity she owed her name of the "Island of the Saints." From the days of St. Patrick the monastic schools, veritable cities of God in the midst of the strife and barbarism of those early days, exerted their influence on the life around them in favour of piety, learning and civilization. Here were being formed a whole population of writers, theologians, architects, sculptors, poets, historians, and above all of missioners and preachers, who were to carry the light of the Gospel far and wide into other lands. The founders of these schools were mostly of the noblest blood in Ireland, and kings and princes did not disdain to come to them for advice and help, or even to listen to their reproofs. Most powerful for good was the influence of the Church in Ireland, and well for her that it was so, for the times were wild and lawless.

To the Hy-Nialls, the kinsmen of Columba, belonged the whole north-west of Ireland. The sovereign rule over the entire country was theirs, in the Irish colony of Dalriada in Caledonia over the seas, as well as in the mother-country of Erin.

They exercised authority over the provincial kings, but an authority that was often hotly contested, and stormily maintained at the cost of much bloodshed. The king was elected from either branch of the great Niall family or clan, the Hy-Nialls of the North, to which Columba belonged, or the Hy-Nialls of the South, and the two branches were continually at war. Into the midst of these discordant elements the law of Christ brought peace and justice, and the Saints of Ireland were the pillars of the law of Christ.

Chapter II

THE SCHOOLING OF A SAINT

WHILE Columba was growing into manhood among the mountains of
Tir-Connell, St. Finnian, "Finnian of the Heart Devout" as the old writers love to call him, was founding his great monastic school of Moville on the northern side of Lough Cuan.

Not on his piety and sanctity alone did the renown of Finnian rest. He had been educated at the famous monastery of Whitehorn, founded by St. Ninian in the fourth century in the British kingdom of Galloway across the sea. St. Ninian was the friend of St. Martin of Tours, and it was from him that he obtained masons to build the Candida Casa or White House, the first stone church erected in Britain. Later, St. Finnian went on pilgrimage to Rome, a difficult and dangerous undertaking in days when ships consisted for the most part of a framework of willow overstretched with ox-hide; and famine, pestilence, wild beasts and barbarians were only a few of the perils that beset travellers by land. There he remained for three months, when he returned to Ireland, bringing with him a precious and priceless treasure.

This was a copy of the sacred Scriptures, translated and corrected by the hand of St. Jerome himself, and formally sanctioned by the Pope as the authentic text. No copy of this first edition of the Vulgate had as yet found its way into Ireland, and to the scholars and scribes of the day it was of untold worth.

The school of Moville was founded in 540, and St. Columba must have been one of its earliest scholars, for he was born in the year 521, and was about twenty years of age when he left Tir-Connell. Here he was ordained deacon, and here also, at his prayer, was worked the first of a long series of miracles that were to continue throughout his life. One festival day, to the consternation of St. Finnian, it was found that there was no wine for the Holy Sacrifice. It was the turn of Columba to draw the water that was to be used in the sacred mysteries, and kneeling at the brink of the well he prayed earnestly to that Lord who had changed water into wine at the marriage feast of Cana to have pity on their distress. His prayer was heard; even as he carried the water to the church the miracle was worked.

"Here, my Father, is wine that God has sent us from heaven," said the young deacon, as he gave the vessel to his master, and Finnian marvelled greatly and gave praise and glory to God.

From Moville, Columba went to the great school of Clonard, there to pursue his studies under another St. Finnian—Finnian the Wise, the "Tutor of the Saints of Erin." Clonard was the most famous school in Ireland at the time, and even bishops and abbots, old in years and experience, did not disdain to come to learn wisdom at the feet of its holy founder. St. Finnian of Clonard had been himself the pupil of three great saints, St. David, St. Gildas, and St. Cadoc, at the College of Llancarvan in Wales. When Columba came to the school of Clonard it numbered, as the old writers tell us, three thousand scholars.

The problem of accommodation was very simple in an Irish school of the sixth century. A few precious manuscripts formed the whole library. The instruction was mostly oral, and given in the green fields round the moat of Clonard. A little hill or eminence formed the professor's chair, and the scholars sat on the slopes about his feet. They built their own little huts of clay and wattles in the surrounding meadows, and took their turn at herding the sheep and grinding in the quern, or handmill, the corn for the daily bread. They prayed and studied, learnt the exquisitely fine transcription that gave to the world the only books that were then to be had, and listened to the interpretation of the Holy Scriptures expounded by St. Finnian with a power and eloquence that drew men from all parts of Ireland to listen.

The son of the Hy-Nialls took his turn with the rest at grinding the corn in the quern and in the humble daily labours, but he accomplished his task so rapidly and skilfully that his fellow-scholars, who may have heard the story of the celestial companion of his boyhood, would assert that he had been helped by an angel. When the daily work was finished, he was always to be found, as of old, before the altar, absorbed in prayer. Even the elders treated him with deference. There was something so noble and commanding in his bearing, so high and holy in the glance of his keen grey eyes, so strong and compelling in the clear tones of his voice, that half unconsciously men bowed before him.

But there was one at Clonard who long withstood his influence. To the gentle-hearted Ciaran "Mac In Tsair," or the son of the carpenter, temptation had come in the shape of an envious thought.

Why should Columba, he asked himself resentfully, be loved and privileged above all the other scholars? He was the son of the Prince of Tir-Connell it was true, but in a monastic community such as Clonard were not they all equal before God? He began to be jealous of the influence exercised so unconsciously by his young companion, and harboured bitterness in his heart. Ciaran's guardian angel grieved over the havoc that was being wrought in that pure and gentle soul. He appeared to him one day in a radiant vision, carrying the tools of a carpenter in his hands.

"See, Ciaran," said he, "what thou hast left for the love of God, to give thyself to Christ in the monastic life; but Columba has sacrificed the throne which would have been his, had he not, forsaking the world, chosen rather to follow his Lord in poverty and humiliation."

His words scattered the mist of envy from the heart of the carpenter's son, who humbly asked pardon for his sin. From henceforth he became one of the warmest friends of Columba, who in his turn loved the gentle-hearted Ciaran with a true and tender affection. It was while the two were at Clonard together that their master St. Finnian dreamt that he saw two moons, one of gold and one of silver, shining in the sky. The golden moon illuminated the north of Ireland, and its beams shone over the sea as far as distant Alba, while the moon of silver shed its soft light in the centre of the land. It was made known to Finnian that the golden moon represented Columba, who was to carry the light of the Gospel to another people, while that of silver typified Ciaran, whose holiness was to be a light to many in his own country.

It was at this time that Columbcille showed the first signs of that gift of prophecy that was to make him so famous in after days.

There came to Clonard an old bard called Gemman, who was a Christian. Columba, who had a passionate love for poetry, put himself under his tuition that he might not only study the old minstrel lore of Ireland, but learn also to pour out his own heart in song. One day when the old man sat reading at a little distance from his pupil in the green meadows near Clonard, a young maiden, crying piteously for help, and hotly pursued by one of the bloodthirsty barbarians who were the terror of the more peaceful inhabitants of the country, fled towards him for protection. Gemman called to Columba for help, but it was too late. Even as he tried to hide the child under the folds of his long cloak her savage assailant pierced her to the heart with his spear.

"How long, O Lord," moaned the old man, as he gathered the body of the little maiden into his arms, "how long shall the blood of this innocent cry unavenged to heaven?"

Columba turned to him with flashing eyes.

"Thus long," he cried in a voice that rang like the trumpet of the avenging angel:

"Thus long, and no longer. The soul of that innocent child shall scarcely have entered heaven before the soul of her murderer shall be cast into eternal fire."

The words had scarcely left his lips when the barbarian, who was not yet out of sight, fell dead, struck down by the sudden judgment of God.

On leaving Clonard, Columba went in company with the gentle-hearted Ciaran to visit the school of another great master of the spiritual life, St. Mobhi of Glasnevin. There they met St. Comgall and St. Cannich, and formed with them a lifelong friendship. It was during his stay at Glasnevin that Columba was sent by St. Mobhi to Etchen, Bishop of Clonfad, to be ordained a priest, and it is characteristic of the simplicity of the times that the holy bishop, who was Columba's own cousin, and the son of a reigning prince, was found in the fields guiding the oxen of his plough.

It must have been also about this time that Ciaran and Columba journeyed together to the rocky Isle of Aran in the west, to visit St. Enda the Holy, the tutor of both Finnian of Moville and Finnian of Clonard. Aran was indeed a very nursery of sanctity, and Enda was reverenced as a father by all the saints of Ireland. They learnt from his lips the virtues and duties of a true monk, but they learnt still more from his example. He and his community slept on the bare ground in their stone cells, never warmed by a fire even in the coldest days of winter. Their frugal food was the fruit of the labour of their hands, but it was little enough that the barren rocks of Aran could furnish. To these men, whose hearts were on fire with the love of God, their desert island was a little paradise, where they lived in close communion with the unseen world, and from whence the voice of praise went up incessantly to the throne of God.

We are told that the gentle-hearted Ciaran, the son of the carpenter, was beloved by Enda above all his disciples, and that when the time came for him to leave the Isle of Aran to found his own great monastery of Clonmacnoise on the banks of the Shannon, the old man knelt and wept bitterly on the rocky shore. Perhaps he may have foreseen the early death of his beloved pupil, the sudden quenching of that light that was to shine so brightly during the few years that remained to him of his earthly pilgrimage.

For a few years after his departure from Aran the holy Ciaran exercised his apostleship in his native country, and then founded the monastery of Clonmacnoise, which in after days was to become the greatest and most learned community in Ireland. Four months later a terrible pestilence broke out, and the gentle Ciaran was amongst its victims. He asked the brethren to take him out into the open air that his eyes might see the blue sky once again before he died. The skin on which he used to sleep was spread on the ground and they laid him on it, weeping bitterly the while. The dying man then asked to be left alone with St. Kevin of Glendalough, his soul's friend (the beautiful old Celtic name for spiritual father—still in use among the Catholics of western Scotland), who blessed him and gave him the Holy Communion.

Ciaran bade him a tender farewell, for, says the old chronicle, he loved him much. Then, lifting his eyes to heaven with a smile on his lips, the pure and holy Ciaran breathed his last, and white angels came and carried his soul to Paradise.

Chapter III

DERRY AND DURROW

THE terrible outbreak of plague that carried off young Ciaran in the flower of his age found Columba at Glasnevin. St. Mobhi bade his disciples disperse to their homes, and Columbcille went northwards to Tir-Connell. When he reached the stream of Moyola he prayed earnestly that God might stay the plague on the southern bank of the river, and spare the country of his people. His prayer was heard, and the terrible scourge forbore to cross the water.

Columba was now twenty-five years of age, and his friends and kinsmen earnestly desired that he should found a church and monastery in their own country. His cousin the Prince of Ailech even offered him a piece of land on the northern coast, but Columba was deaf to their entreaties. His master, St. Mobhi, had given him no permission to found; and without it, so great was his reverence for the holy old man, he would take no steps in the matter. But Mobhi had fallen a victim to the pestilence and was sick unto death. One of his last acts was to send messengers in search of his beloved disciple, to take him his blessing and his girdle in token that the time had come for him to found his monastery.

The spot that Ailech had offered to Columba was altogether after his own heart and was now most gratefully accepted. The so-called "island" of Derry or Daire, surrounded as it was on two sides by the Foyle water and on the third by a marsh, consisted of a gently rising green hill, crowned on the summit with a beautiful wood of oaks. So dear was the oak grove of Derry to Columbcille, that rather than cut down one of its trees, he preferred to build his church in the space that remained between them.

The cells of the monks were placed at the foot of the hill by the water's edge, and it was not long before the young men of Tir-Connell came flocking to Daire to give themselves to the service of God under the rule of their young kinsman.

It was in this beloved church of Derry that it was given so often to Columba to behold the angels adoring their Lord on His altar throne, and to hear the melody of their voices as they sang the eternal song of praise.

Prayer, labour, and study divided the hours of the day, and young as was the abbot, the hand that governed, though gentle, was very firm. Columba had learnt from his holy masters in the spiritual life to lead his monks by example even more than by precept. He slept on the bare ground, with a skin for covering and a stone for pillow. Three times in the night he rose to pray, and his food was of the scantiest and poorest description. "Though my devotion is great," he would say, "I sit in a chair of glass, for I am frail and fleshly." No work was too menial for him, and he would carry the sacks of grain on his strong shoulders from the mill to the kitchen like the humblest brother. His austerities were the admiration of his monks, who strove in all things to follow the example set before them.

Of all the foundations of Columba, and we are told of no less than thirty-seven, Derry was the one that remained always the dearest to his heart, and many of the sweet songs of his making celebrate its praises.

The reason I love Daire is
For its peace and its purity,
And for its crowds of white angels
From one end to the other.

My Daire, my little oak grove,
My dwelling, my dear little cell;
O Eternal God in Heaven above,
Woe be to him who violates it,

sings the Saint in the soft Erse or Gaelic of his native land. "On every leaf of the oaks of Derry," he would say, "there sits a white angel listening to the brethren as they sing the praises of God."

The dear oak trees of Derry were never to be cut down, and if one were uprooted by the storm it was to lie for nine days before it was divided between the poor and the guest-house of the monastery.

There was a hamlet on the northern side of the hill, and a hundred poor were fed every day by the monks of Derry. Once during a thunderstorm some of the wretched little houses caught tire. The people hastened to

Columba, who went at once to the church. There with outstretched arms he poured forth his soul in supplication before the altar, and the fire ceased at his prayer.

A fragment of the rule in use amongst the old Celtic monasteries has been preserved, in which we can see the spirit of the monks of Columba's time:

"Yield submission to every rule—that is devotion.

"A mind prepared for red martyrdom—that is death for the faith.

"A mind fortified and steadfast for white martyrdom—that is the trials and mortifications and crosses of earthly life.

"Forgiveness from the heart to everyone.

"Constant prayers for those who trouble thee.

"Love God with all thy heart and all thy strength, and love thy neighbour as thyself."

Strong and simple, like the saints of the time, to whom the "red martyrdom" might come at any moment, and to whose fiery natures the forgiveness of injuries was not always the easiest of precepts.

But Derry, with its oak grove and its angels, was not the only spot that was dear to Columba.

Foremost in his affections amongst the other religious houses of his founding was Durrow—in Irish Dair-nagh, or the plain of oaks. It was also known as Druin-Cain, or "the beautiful hill," and well did it deserve its name. The land, as was the case with so many of the old monasteries, had been given to Columba by a reigning prince, probably a kinsman of his own. Of Durrow the story is told that there was in the orchard of the monastery an apple tree noted for the abundance as well as the bitterness of its fruit. But Columbcille blessed the tree, and thenceforward, says the old chronicle, its apples became sweet and good.

While Columba was at Durrow he wrote the celebrated copy of the Gospels known as the "Book of Durrow." An ardent lover of the Sacred Scriptures, and a skilful and patient scribe, he is said to have written with his own hand no less than thirty copies of the Gospels and the Psalter. The "Book of Durrow" is a transcription of the four Gospels, exquisitely illuminated with the intricate designs of the Celtic school. On the back is to be deciphered a petition for prayers from "Columba the scribe, who wrote this evangel in the space of twelve days."

The poet-saint could sing the charms of Durrow as well as those of Derry:

> There the wind sings through the oaks and the elms,
> The joyous note of the blackbird is heard at dawn,
> The cuckoo chants from tree to tree in that noble land.

And again he calls it:
> A city devout with its hundred crosses,
> Without blemish and without transgression.

In the years to come, when Columba was in Iona, one cold winter's day the brethren noticed that their beloved abbot was sad and silent.

"What ails you, Father?" asked Diarmaid, his faithful companion.

"My soul is sorrowful," said Columbcille, "for my dear monks of Durrow. Bitter is the weather, and their abbot keeps them hard at work, fasting and a-cold."

At the same moment Laisren, the abbot of Durrow, felt a sudden inspiration to bid his monks get their dinner, and take a little rest, on account of the severity of the weather. Another day about the same time, when the monks of Durrow were building their new church, Columba in his cell at Iona saw one of them falling from the roof. He cried to God for help, and his guardian angel—such is the flashlike speed of an angel's flight—caught the monk ere he touched the ground.

More famous even than the "Book of Durrow" is the celebrated "Book of Kells," the most wonderful monument of the art of the Sixth Century that has come down to us. It was written also by the hand of Columbcille for Kells, his third foundation, though some of the illustrations were probably added at a later date.

The story runs that not long after the foundation of Durrow, Columba went to Kells, one of the royal seats of Diarmaid, High King of Ireland. Now Diarmaid belonged to the southern branch of the Hy-Nialls and was regarded by the northern branch with no great favour. When Columba arrived the King was absent, and the Saint was treated with scant ceremony by the soldiers of the royal guard, to whom he was probably a stranger. When Diarmaid returned and heard of the insult that had been offered in his royal palace to the greatest and most beloved of the Saints of Erin, one of the royal blood and his own cousin, he was ready to make atonement by any means in his power. He offered to give Columba Kells itself and the surrounding country for the founding of a monastery and a church.

It is possible that Diarmaid, whose seat on the throne was anything but secure at the time, was not unmoved by the thought that the powerful clan of the Hy-Nialls of Tir-Connell would not be slow in avenging the insult to one of their clan. However that may be, Columba accepted the gift with gratitude, and so the monastery and the church of Kells came to be built.

The great Gospel of Columbcille, or the "Book of Kells," has been the admiration of all ages. The patience and the delicate skill required for such an undertaking is to be wondered at. Certainly the old monks believed that if a thing were worth doing at all it was worth doing well, particularly if that thing happened to be a copy of the Gospels of Christ.

The untiring zeal and the labours of Columba had indeed brought forth fruit throughout the whole country. His friends and kinsfolk were generous, and churches and monasteries built by the Saint and owning him as their patron and head sprang up in every direction. Derry, Durrow, Kells, Raphoe, Sords, Drumcliff, Kilmacrenan, Drumcolumb, Glencolumbcille are but a few of his foundations. More than ever might it have been said of St. Columba that he was beloved of God and of man.

But God shows His love for His Saints in ways which are not the ways of men, and the chastening fires of sorrow and of suffering were to purify that ardent and impulsive nature. The haughty spirit of the descendant of Niall of the Nine Hostages had yet to be conformed to that of his great Master Who is meek and humble of heart.

Chapter IV

THE COW AND THE CALF

WE have already spoken of the pilgrimage to Rome of St. Finnian of Moville, and of the treasure that he had brought back with him from over the sea—a copy of the Scriptures translated and corrected by the hand of the great St. Jerome himself. Columba, when at Moville, must often have seen and perhaps even have handled the precious volume. In later days, so great was his desire that each of his monasteries should have its copy of the Word of God, that he would seek out and transcribe with his own hand all the most carefully written and most authentic manuscripts to be found in Ireland.

The love of these old books, regarded by the Saints of Ireland as their most precious treasure, amounted almost to a passion with Columba, so that we are hardly surprised to find him journeying to Moville to ask permission from his old master to make a copy of his rare and valuable manuscript. But he was met by an unexpected rebuff; St. Finnian guarded his treasure with a jealous eye, and feared to trust it in any hands but his own. He firmly refused the request of his old pupil, and no entreaties of Columba could move him from his decision. But the determination of Columbcille was equal to his own, and he resolved to obtain the object of his desire in spite of St. Finnian's prohibition.

He waited until all had gone to rest, and then, armed with parchment and pigments, went softly to the church, where the precious book was kept. Night after night, in spite of weary hand and eye, he laboured at his self-imposed task until the day broke, and men began to stir. To undertake the transcription of the whole book would have been an impossibility, working thus secretly in the night; he therefore confined himself to copying the Psalter. To Columba, poet as he was by nature, the psalms of the "sweet singer of Israel" were particularly clear, and the wording of the new version gave the force and the melody of the original more perfectly than any rendering up till then in use.

The lonely vigils in the church passed quickly, in spite of the weariness that assailed but could not daunt the enthusiastic scribe. One night, one of the scholars of Moville, happening to pass the door of the church, was astonished to see a bright light shining through the crevices of the door. He stooped and looked through the keyhole. Keyholes as well as keys were on a large scale in the sixth century, and he obtained a good view of the interior, and of Columba bending over the reading desk with a pile of parchment before him, copying with skilful hand the treasure of Moville. The whole chancel was shining with a brilliant light which fell directly across the page on which the writer was at work.

The young man, awestruck at the sight, crept softly away, and warned his master of what was taking place. St. Finnian knew Columba's skill in transcription. He made no move until the Psalter was completed, and his old pupil was preparing to depart. Then he accused his guest of having taken a copy of his book without his permission and against his will, and claimed the work as his rightful property.

This was to touch Columba in a tender spot. His nocturnal labours had cost him many weary vigils, but he had borne the weariness gladly for the sake of the prize—to give up the fruit of so much toil was more than could be expected of him. He flatly refused to yield to Finnian's claim. The old man was determined; Columba was firm; neither would give way. It was agreed in the end to appeal to the King at Tara, and to hold his judgment as final. Diarmaid might be considered as a fit judge in such a matter. The friend and patron of the great monastery of Clonmacnoise, founded by Ciaran in his presence and with his help, the King was looked upon by all the Saints of Ireland as their friend. Moreover, he was Columba's own cousin, and had treated him on a former occasion with reverence and consideration. Columba himself had no doubt that the judgment would be in his favour, and went readily at Finnian's suggestion to lay the matter before him.

But Diarmaid's position on the throne was more secure than it had been in former days. He may have thought that he had less reason to fear the enmity of the Hy-Nialls of Tir-Connell. He had heard much of the sanctity of Columba, and may have supposed that in spite of his high lineage he would be ready to bear with patience an adverse judgment. He may have been actuated by the old enmity between the two branches of the family; or he may have decided according to his own conscience as he thought right and just. Be that as it may, the judgment came as a thunderclap to Columbcille.

"To every cow," said the King, "belongs its own calf." Since the copy of Columba was the "son-book" of the manuscript of Moville, it belonged by rights to its mother, and therefore to Finnian.

Columba's indignation knew no bounds. The judgment was unfair and unjust, he declared; Diarmaid should bear the penalty. With dashing eyes and burning heart he turned his back on King and courtiers, and strode from the royal presence.

He was now a man with a grievance, who considered that he had been most unjustly treated, but the resentment which was as yet but smouldering in his heart was soon to be fanned into a flame.

It came to pass that Diarmaid made a great feast at Court and invited all the princes and nobles of Erin to attend. Games were held for several days in the green meadows of Tara, that the young athletes might show their skill in wrestling. Now brawling and quarrelling at these royal games had been strictly forbidden by the King on account of the serious accidents that had happened on former occasions. But the blood of young Ireland was hot and undisciplined, and in a moment of anger, Curnan, the heir of the Prince of Connaught, struck the son of the King's steward and felled him to the ground. The act was altogether unpremeditated, but the blow had struck the lad in a vital spot; when they tried to raise him, they found that he was dead. Young Curnan dared not face the wrath of Diarmaid, and fled for protection to Columba, who was his kinsman.

It was an acknowledged thing that an abbot or the founder of a religious house had the right to give sanctuary even to great criminals, and the claim was universally respected. But Diarmaid was very angry and sent messengers who dragged the boy from the very presence of Columba and`put him to death on the spot.

This fresh insult was more than Columbcille could bear. The rights of the Church had been violated in his person. His own people, the Hy-Nialls of the north, should judge between him and Diarmaid, he declared, and set forth on his journey northwards, breathing vengeance as he went. The King himself was not a little apprehensive as to what might be the results of his arbitrary action; he stationed guards on all the roads that led northwards, and even tried to detain the fugitive in prison. But Columbcille successfully evaded the traps that had been set to catch him, and by a lonely path across the mountains went his way to Tir-Connell. As he journeyed he sang a song of confidence in the God in whom he trusted to protect the right.

> I am alone upon the mountain
> Do Thou, O God, protect my path.
> Then shall I have no fear,
> Though six thousand men were against me.
> What protection shall guard thee from death?
> The Son of Mary shall cause thee to prosper.
> The King who has made our bodies
> He it is in whom I believe.
> My Lord is Christ the Son of God,
> Christ, the Son of Mary, the great abbot,
> Father, Son and Holy Ghost.

So singing he went speedily and in safety to his own country, where he recounted his wrongs to the men of his own race.

Aedh, Prince of Connaught, the father of the lad who had been so cruelly put to death, was already preparing for vengeance. The chiefs of Tir-Connell joined him, hot in Columba's cause. The men who gathered to avenge the insult made a formidable army, and Diarmaid on his side lost no time in gathering his forces for battle.

The encounter took place at Cuil-dreimhne, between Balbulbin Mountain and the sea, and the fight was long and bloody. Columba, say some of the old writers, was himself present, and prayed with outstretched arms for the victory of his people.

Three thousand of Diarmaid's men fell on the field of battle, while the losses of the Hy-Nialls of the north, such was the efficacy of the prayers of Columbcille, were comparatively slight. The victory was complete, but Diarmaid was not the man to take his defeat meekly.

He appealed to the Church to judge the conduct of Columba. Did it seem right and good, he asked, that a priest and an abbot, the founder of religious houses, and one who had dedicated his life to the service of Christ, should have provoked a bloody war which had been the death of thousands of innocent men? The churchmen looked grave. The case thus stated did not promise well for Columba.

He was the friend of all: the zeal and fervour of his life, the charity and generosity of his heart were known throughout the length and breadth of Erin. There was but one weak point in that noble nature—the haughty spirit that had come to him with the hot blood of the Hy-Nialls; and certainly he had been sorely tried by circumstances. Yet—the fact was incontestable—his conduct as an abbot and as a priest was open to the gravest censure. He was ordered to appear before an ecclesiastical council which was summoned to meet at Teilte in the heart of the King's domains to hear the judgment that should be pronounced upon him by the Saints of Erin.

Chapter V

A BITTER PENANCE

MANY of the holiest men in Ireland were present at the Synod of Teilte. St. Enda of Aran had passed from his life of penance to the glory which is eternal; but St. Brendan of Birr, and probably his namesake the Bishop of Clonfert, with his assistant St. Moinen, Oena of Clonmacnoise, successor of the saintly Ciaran, and St. Kevin of Glendalough, formed part of the Council.

When Columba was seen approaching in the distance, St. Brendan of Birr alone arose and went forward to receive him. The Fathers objected to his action. It was not fitting, they said, that one who was under the grave censure of the Church should be greeted with marks of deference and honour.

"If you saw what I see," replied the holy Brendan, "you would hasten to do likewise. I see Columba, as he climbs the hill, surrounded by a column of light, and angels going before and after him. I bow before the Hand of God which destines him to convert a whole nation to the faith of Christ."

His words made a powerful impression on the assembly, for the wisdom of Brendan was known to all; and there was a deep silence as Columba entered.

After a short pause one of the elders arose and stated the case in words that were brief and simple. Columba, he said, was under the censure of his brethren for having stirred up strife in the King's dominions, which had led to a fierce and bloody battle.

"The King's behaviour was unjust," replied Columba, "and it is hard for a man to bear injustice patiently."

"Truly, as you say," answered the speaker, "it is hard for a man to bear injustice; yet judge yourself if it is more fitting that one who has dedicated his life to the service of Christ should bear injuries patiently, or that he should avenge them at the point of the sword." He went on to speak of the duties of a Christian and of a priest; of the insults and humiliations offered to Jesus Christ, their Master and their model. The words were of one who had himself striven and conquered—of one who had a right to speak. The silence deepened, for the Spirit of God was with him.

Alone in their midst stood Columba, but his head was bowed upon his breast, and the grey eyes that had dashed so stormily at the Court of Tara were dim with tears. The cry that burst from his heart when the old man ceased to speak was the cry of another great penitent—one who in spite of human frailty had deserved to be called a "man after God's own heart."

"Against Thee only have I sinned and done this evil in Thy sight: For I acknowledge my fault, and my sin is ever before me."

The fault had been great, but the sincerity of the repentance was evident to all.

"Go in peace," was the verdict of the Council, "and for every man that fell on the field of Cuil-dreimhne win a soul to the faith of Christ."

Sentence had been given, but Columba was not content. He had grieved that Lord Who from his childhood had been the sole love of his heart, and no penance was great enough to satisfy him. Moreover the fate of the men who had fallen at Cuil-dreimhne was an intolerable burden on his soul. Through his fault they had been hurried—perhaps altogether unprepared—before the judgment-seat of God. The thought that they might be lost for all eternity was a perpetual torture to him, and he went from one to another of the Saints of Erin seeking advice and help.

In due time he went to St. Abban, like himself a monk, and the founder of many religious houses. Men called him the "Peacemaker," such was his power over turbulent and violent men. Not long before, he had gone alone and unarmed to meet one of the fiercest barbarians of the land, the heathen chief of a reigning clan, and the terror of the surrounding country. Such was the influence of Abban that the marauder laid down his arms, and became in course of time not only a Christian, but also a monk of exceptionally holy life.

Columba found St. Abban in the Church of one of his religious foundations, known amongst the people as the "Cell of Tears" on account of the contrition of the penitents who frequented it. He besought the holy abbot to pray for the souls of those who through his fault had met their death, and the thought of whose fate had destroyed his peace. He entreated Abban also to pray to God that He would reveal to him through the angel who spoke to him continually of the things of heaven, whether they were saved or lost.

The humility of the holy abbot would not allow him for a long time to accede to this last request; but in the end, so moved was he by the anguish of Columba, that he fell on his knees and implored of God to give this comfort to a soul in pain. The knowledge that he asked was given him; he returned with great joy to his visitor to tell him that, through the infinite mercy of God, the souls of all who had fallen on that fatal day had been saved. The chief solicitude of Columba was now at rest, but the future was not yet clear before him. How was he to mould his life that the days to come might be an atonement for the fault that was past? He had learnt his own weakness, he must lean more than ever on the Strength that cannot fail, and the desire for a more perfect expiation was strong in his heart. He determined to seek out St. Molaise, his "soul's friend," in the lonely isle of Inishmurry and to ask his counsel.

St. Molaise knew well the character of his penitent. The penance that would satisfy that great heart must be full and complete. To Columba the love of country came next to the love of God; the decision was taken ere the penitent had ceased to speak.

It had been decreed, said he, by the Synod that Columba was to win to the faith of Christ as many men as had perished at the battle of Cuil-dreimhne. Let him do so; but that the atonement might be more perfect let him go forth from his own people and his own land, and never look upon the hills of Erin again.

Columba bowed his head before the sentence. "It shall be done," he answered, and none but God was to know what the doing cost him. It only remained to break the news to his friends and kinsfolk. A wail of sorrow rang through Tir-Connell at the tidings.

It is not surprising that the land of Alba over the sea suggested itself at once to Columba as the place of his exile. The little kingdom of Dalriada on the Argyllshire coast was ruled by one of his own kinsmen, and reports of the condition of the surrounding country had possibly reached his ears. The Christianity introduced by St. Ninian two hundred years before had almost disappeared. The ruling chiefs were completely under the influence of the Druids, and heathenism and idolatry were supreme throughout the land. There his apostolic spirit would be able to find ample scope. We are told by some of the old writers that the thought of a missionary journey to Caledonia had been for years one of his dearest projects. If that were so, the time had now come to put it into execution.

Columba chose the companions who were to share in his great undertaking from amongst the monks of Derry. Two cousins of his own, Baithen, who was to succeed him in after years as abbot of Iona, and his brother Cobthach, were amongst the number. But the disciple who loved him the most was Mochonna, son of the King of Ulster, whom Columba considered too young for an enterprise that involved so many dangers, and to whose entreaties he refused to yield. It was not fitting, said he, that the young monk should leave the country of his birth and the parents to whom he was so dear; but Mochonna would not be gainsaid.

"Thou," he cried, "art the father of my soul, and Holy Church is my mother, and my country is the spot where I can work most fruitfully for Christ."

Then, that it might be impossible for his beloved master to leave him behind, he made a vow before all who were present to quit his native land and to follow Columba to the death. It was in this wise that the determined and devoted Mochonna overcame all opposition and obtained his heart's desire. He was to become one of the most active and zealous of the little band of missionaries, in Alba, where he was venerated for many centuries under the name of St. Machor, as the patron and founder of the See of Aberdeen.

Thus, with only twelve companions, in the wicker-work "curraghs" covered with oxhide that were the only boats of the Celtic races at the time, the future apostle of Scotland set sail from his native land. A great crowd, gathered from all the surrounding country, stood on the shore, and as the light skiffs sped out into the sea, and the green hill of Derry faded slowly from the eyes of the mariners, the sound of a bitter wailing was borne to them on the breeze. The best beloved of the Saints of Erin had left her, and she mourned for him as one lost to her for ever.

Chapter VI

THE ISLE IN THE WESTERN SEAS

IT must have taken the little band of missionaries, even if the wind were in their favour, fully a day to make the coast of "Calyddon" or "the Land of Forests," as Scotland was then called by the Britons south of the Clyde.

They landed first, we are told, on the island of Oronsay, but on climbing a hill to look out over the waste of waters, Columba caught sight of the far faint coast of Ireland lying like a blue cloud on the horizon. It was more than he could bear, and the mariners put out to sea again, sailing northwards till they reached the little island of Hy or Iona, off the coast of Mull. (Hy or Hii means "the island"; Iona "the blessed island.") The bay where they landed still bears the name of Port'a Curraigh or "the Bay of the Wicker Boat." No trace of the hills of Erin was to be seen from the low-lying rocks of Iona, nothing but the blue mountains and the dark crags of the Hebrides and the white-capped waves of the sea. Here, therefore, the ambassadors of Christ resolved to build their little monastery and to make their home.

It was a happy choice. No better quarters could have been found for a missionary station. Iona, separated only by a narrow channel from the island of Mull, lay exactly opposite to the friendly kingdom of Dalriada, and the missionaries had only to sail up the chain of lochs, now united by artificial means and called the Caledonian Canal, to find themselves in the heathen country of the Picts. The weird and austere beauty of the Hebrides with their wild rocks and foaming seas did not at first appeal to the Gaels of Ireland, fresh from the green hills and smiling landscapes of their native land. The bare crags and the dark mountains, the grey skies and the hollow waves that beat perpetually on those bleak shores,

and bring The eternal note of sadness in,

the wailing of the wind through the caves and the narrow channels fretted into weird shapes by the ocean tide, made a music which was alien to their ears, and strangely melancholy to their warm Irish hearts. Again and again the passionate note of longing for the dear mother-country breaks out in the writings of Columba.

> 'Twere sweet to sail the white waves that break on the shores of Erin,
> 'Twere sweet to land 'mid the white foam that laps on the shores of Erin,
> My boat would fly were its prow once turned to the dear land of Erin,
> And the sad heart cease to bleed.

> There's a grey eye that ever turns with longing look to Erin,
> No more in life again to see the men and maids of Erin.
> There's a mist of tears in the melting eye that sadly turns to Erin,
> Where the birds' songs are so sweet.

Hy, he calls the "land of ravens"; it was only after many years that he was to sing of the place of his exile as

> Hy of my love, Hy of my heart,

dear then as the land of his labours and of his apostolate for Christ, and very close in his affections to the country of his birth.

The poet-heart of Columbcille could sing of his regret for the island of his birth; but he was not the man to let it interfere with his work for God in the island of his adoption. Iona consisted for the most part of barren and desert moor. Columba asked and obtained it as a gift from Conal, King of the Dalriadan Scots, and set his monks at once to cultivate the soil. The huts of the brethren were built in a circle round the church, with a guest-house and a simple refectory adjoining. The building was of wood and wattles, and the work proceeded rapidly. The hut of Columba was in the most elevated spot of the monastic enclosure, and here, during the short intervals between his missionary journeys, he spent his time in prayer, study, and the transcription of the Holy Scriptures. Iona had its writing school for the training of the younger monks, and became famous later for the excellence of its scribes. Adamnan in his Life of St. Columba mentions the scriptorium with its waxen tablets and the styles for writing, the inkhorns and the pens, with the brushes and the colours for illuminating the manuscripts.

In all the labours of the day Columba took his part; no work was too humble for the holy abbot, and he exacted from others the same cheerful diligence as he himself practised. No one was allowed to be idle, there was work enough for all, and each was expected to take his share. When the manual labours were ended for the day, the monks betook themselves to prayer, reading, or writing, while the less expert could always employ themselves in works of charity for the common good. Even while the brethren were engaged in active labour, they strove to occupy their minds with thoughts of God, so that their work might be hallowed by prayer and bring its blessings on their mission. When the toils of the day were at an end they took their rest on their hard pallets of straw; but Columba slept on the bare ground with a stone for pillow, as had been his custom from his earliest years.

The rule of a Celtic community recommended hospitality to guests as strongly as personal austerity, and nowhere was this rule more faithfully observed than at Iona. No sooner were the monks settled in their new home, than pilgrims came from every quarter to ask counsel of Columba or to embrace the religious life under his direction. The holy abbot, who sought in every action of his life to make atonement by true humility for the movement of pride that had cost him so dear, would go himself to meet them. Kneeling before them he would loosen their sandals and wash their feet, which he kissed with reverent devotion; performing for them, in imitation of his Divine Master, this lowliest of services. At every hour of the day or night shouts might be heard across the narrow channel that divided Iona from the island of Mull. At this signal the brethren would leave their work to go down to the shore where, stepping into their "curraghs," they would row across the Sound to fetch the pilgrims.

Some of these were merely moved by a desire to see and speak to the holy man whose fame had already reached their ears. Some were in need of advice, some of material help. Some had a load of sin and sorrow on their souls, and desired the Saint's absolution; some were suffering from diseases, and sought his prayers and blessing; while others wished to leave the world and join the brethren in their life of penance. There was no sorrow to which the loving sympathy of Columbcille did not extend, no necessity which did not appeal to his charity. He dealt with them all in turn, and gave to each according to his need.

It was on one of these occasions that Columba, engaged at the moment in transcribing the Scriptures, foretold sadly that one of the pilgrims who was heard shouting lustily on the seashore, would shortly upset his inkhorn. The visitor, a too enthusiastic admirer, in his eagerness to embrace the Saint, fulfilled the prediction to the letter. Luckily the sleeve of Columba's tunic was the only thing that suffered. He had probably put the precious manuscript in a place of safety.

He was careful with those who desired to embrace the religious life, and would make trial of their vocation with wise severity. He knew well that in those wild days it was no uncommon thing for men who had led evil lives to desire to make atonement for their sins in a monastery. Given that the repentance were sincere, he wholly approved their design, for many of the Saints of the Church have been converted sinners. But he knew also the weakness of human nature and the strength of the evil habits of a lifetime, and demanded that such penitents should go through a long probation and prove their sincerity by humility and obedience to those in charge of them before they were admitted to the religious life.

For these would-be monks he founded communities on some of the neighbouring islands, where wise and saintly men might try their virtue by a probation which lasted sometimes for seven years or even longer when necessary.

On one occasion when Columba was visiting one of these foundations on the island of Himba, he ordered that in honour of his presence, some savoury addition should be made to the frugal midday meal. The brethren gratefully partook of the holiday fare in the spirit in which it was given—with one exception. This was one of the penitents who was undergoing his probation and who seemed to think it more perfect to refuse the proffered dainty. Columba with kindly insistence offered the dish with his own hands to the reluctant brother, and pressed him to partake of it, thinking that some scruple might be distressing him. But he was met with an abrupt refusal. For a moment Columbcille was silent, then looking at the man sternly he said: "You refuse the comfort which I and your superior think it right to offer you. The time will come when you will become a thief again as you were of old, and will steal venison for your own pleasure in the forests of your native place." The prophecy was fulfilled. Not long after, the man returned to his evil life, and died unrepentant in his own country.

In spite of these precautions the community at Iona increased so rapidly that the island soon became too small to hold it, and little bands of devoted men were sent forth to found other monasteries on the mainland, to spread the faith and love of Christ. There are more than ninety churches in Scotland that can trace their foundation to the time of Columba; and each church, according to the custom of the time, had its neighbouring monastery.

The first missionary journey of Columba was to the Scots of Dalriada. They were Christians it is true, but living as they did surrounded on all sides by a heathen population, they were apt to be influenced more or less by the customs of their neighbours. It was necessary that friendly relations should be established with these men, themselves originally of Irish extraction, before attempting the conversion of the Picts. The monks of Iona were hardy mariners as well as tillers of the soil. The holy island had its little fleet of curraghs which varied in size according to the number of ox-hides used in their construction. In these frail barks the missionaries would brave the stormy seas of the Hebrides and all the dangers of the deep, secure in their trust in God and the prayers of their holy abbot. There were sharks, and whales too, on the coasts of Caledonia in those days, and the curraghs were small protection against such monsters; but the hearts of the mariners were stout and their faith was strong. They sailed northwards to far St. Kilda and the Orkney and Shetland Isles, where the ruins are still to be seen of churches which they founded.

The holy abbot would take his turn at the oars with the rest, and when he was not with the missioners on their travels would follow them in spirit from his cell at Iona, shielding and protecting them by his prayers. He knew by the supernatural light that God had given him when they were in danger, and suffered with them in all the hardships they endured. The interests of the last and least of them were as dear to him as his own. Small wonder then that the memory of the holy life lived more than thirteen hundred years ago is fragrant and living still, and that the name of Columba is cherished in the land of his adoption even to the present day.

Chapter VII

THE APOSTLE OF SCOTLAND

IN the mountain fastnesses of Caledonia beyond the Grampian Hills, lived a wild and hardy race of men known to their British neighbours as the Picts or "Painted People." The name had originally been bestowed on them by the Romans in allusion to their habit of going into battle with their bodies tattooed all over with strange devices. They were a brave and warlike tribe, who had resisted the landing of Agricola and his legions, and after several pitched battles had driven the Roman eagles triumphantly before them to the sea. In later days they became the terror of the Britons of Strathclyde and Northumbria, descending upon them in wild hordes and raiding their country without mercy. These men were the original ancestors of the Highlanders of Scotland, in whom the courage and the fighting spirit, typical of the race, have survived through all the vicissitudes of their country, and who to this day are acknowledged to be the bravest and hardiest of the soldiers of the Empire.

It was to this people, like himself of Celtic origin, that Columba was to carry the priceless gift of the faith, entering with a handful of unarmed men into the heart of the country which the Roman legions had feared to penetrate. Brude or Bmidh, the Pictish King, was entrenched in his fortress on a rocky hill near the site of Inverness. The little band of missionaries wound their way up the hill, chanting as they went a psalm of confidence in God. At their head was Columba, bearing aloft the cross. The tidings of their approach was brought to the Pictish King, who ordered that the gates of the fortress should be barred against them and admittance refused.

Broichem, the high-priest of the Druids, the foster-father and chief adviser of King Brude, was probably responsible for the order, for, the Christians once admitted, he feared that his influence would be no longer supreme. Columba, however, was not in the least daunted by this inhospitable reception. He made the sign of the Cross before the barred gates and struck them strongly with his clenched fist. Bolts and bars shot back at his touch, and silently the great gates rolled open to give the Saint and his companions passage. The King, who had seen the marvel together with all his Court, was struck with fear, and went to meet Columba with fair and peaceful words. From henceforth he treated him with reverence and courtesy, confirming to him the gift of Iona, which might be considered to lie as much in his territory as in that of the Dalriadan king, and remaining throughout his lifetime a true friend and protector.

It was not until some time later that he became a Christian, but the Druids could foresee the results of his friendly intercourse with the missionaries, and resolved not to lose their influence without a struggle. Their bitter enmity was to follow Columba for years, and to be the chief hindrance to his work amongst the Picts.

The religion of the Druids of Caledonia differed in some degree from that of the Druids of Britain. The people were taught to worship the sun, the rivers and the forests. Certain of the streams and wells which were, said the Druid priests, under the influence of a beneficent spirit, were wholesome and good to drink, while to taste of others which they declared to be under the rule of evil spirits, would be followed by instant death.

The first thing to be done was to convince the people of the falsity of their belief and to make them cease the idolatrous practices connected with it. Columba drank in their presence of the water that was supposed to be deadly, to prove to them that no evil effects would follow. The Druids pursued him wherever he went, interrupting him continually in his preaching, holding him up to the derision of the people, and misrepresenting what he said. Columba bore all their insults with patience; but when it came to trying to drown the missionaries' voices in the singing of the psalms of the Church with shouts and mocking cries, his zeal for God's glory overcame for once his meekness, and he intoned the holy chant in such a voice of thunder that his adversaries were silenced, and the King and his people trembled with fear.

In spite of the Druids, crowds flocked to hear the preaching of Columba, and many were converted to the faith. On one occasion, shortly after the conversion to Christianity of a whole family, the eldest son fell ill and died. The Druids were of course at hand to assure the sorrowing father that the loss of his child was a well-merited punishment indicted by the gods of his country in consequence of his apostasy. The man's faith wavered, but

Columba was watching over his converts; and after doing what he could to console the grief of the boy's parents, asked to be left alone beside the bier to pray. With tears and entreaties he besought of God to show forth His almighty power, and the Heavenly Father heard the prayer of His servant and raised the child to life. Columba led him to his parents, and their faith in the true God was confirmed for ever. The prayer of Columbcille, says Adamnan his biographer, was as powerful with God as that of Elias and Eliseus in the old law, and Peter, John, and Paul in the new.

One day when the Saint was preaching the Gospel in the island of Skye, he had one of those flashes of supernatural insight of which we have spoken several times before. He told his companions that there would come to them that very day an old Pictish chief who was at the point of death, and who had tried to lead a good life according to the natural law of God and the light of his own conscience.

It happened as he had foretold. Towards evening a boat was seen approaching the coast of Skye, manned by Pictish warriors supporting in their arms an old man whose trappings proclaimed him to be of noble birth. Drawing their boat to the shore, they landed and formed a rude litter with their shields, on which they carried the old chieftain up the hill and laid him down at Columba's feet. The Saint spoke to the dying man of the faith of Christ and baptized him, and shortly afterwards he gave up his soul to God.

On another occasion when they were crossing the mountains, Columba saw a vision of angels, and exhorted his companions to hasten on their way. "For," said he, "there is a man of good and honest life waiting beyond the hills to receive baptism before he dies." They quickened their pace, and when they reached Glen Urquhart, found, as Columba had predicted, an old man awaiting their arrival. The holy abbot baptized him and bade him depart in peace, and the angels whom he had seen on the mountains carried his soul to heaven.

The chief Druid Broichem had a young Irish slave-girl, taken captive in time of war, for whose freedom Columba had several times petitioned. The Druid, who was not likely to look favourably on any request of the great Christian missionary, even refused to accept the ransom offered for the girl, though she was pining her heart out for her family and her home.

Columbcille warned him that if he persistently refused to show mercy to his captive, the punishment of God would overtake him, and he would die before Columba himself left the country, but Broichem was not to be moved. Not long afterwards Columba set out on his return journey to Iona, but he had hardly reached Loch Ness when he was overtaken by two messengers from the high-priest beseeching him to take pity on their master, who had been suddenly taken ill and was in danger of death.

They were assured that the Druid would recover, but only on condition that he set the Irish maiden at liberty. She was at once sent to Columba, who found means for her return to her country and her people. As for Broichem, he was more incensed than ever against the Christians, and considered how he could best check their growing influence with the people.

The Druids seem to have had a certain power over the elements, perhaps through the evil spirits whom they worshipped. They had heard of and seen the miracles worked by Columba, and resolved to show how superior their powers of magic were to his.

On the day fixed for the departure of the missionaries, Broichem threatened that he would cause a thick fog and a contrary wind to arise, so that it would be impossible for them to embark.

The people were gathered in crowds to bid farewell to Columba, when to their great consternation the Druid's threat was fulfilled. The fog was dense and the unfavourable wind blew stormily. This time at least they had triumphed, or so they thought, and they did not attempt to conceal their joy.

But Columba, nothing daunted, bade the mariners spread their sails, and the awe-stricken crowd on the shore beheld the boat flying swiftly westwards to Iona in the teeth of the contrary wind, as if it had been altogether in their favour.

The departure was not to be for long. Again and again Columba revisited the mainland to strengthen and confirm the faith of his converts; and in course of time churches and monasteries sprang up amongst the forests and the mountains of Caledonia, little strongholds of Christianity the beneficent influence of which was soon to penetrate throughout the length and breadth of the land.

Columba had many faithful helpers in his missionary labours. Malruve, a kinsman and countryman of his own, soon followed him to Iona to share in his work among the Picts. He became abbot of Appercrossan, now Applecross, on the north-west coast of Caledonia, and suffered the "red martyrdom" some years after the death of Columbcille, at the hands of Norwegian pirates. St. Canice, the companion of Columba and Ciaran at Clonard and Glasnevin, also followed his old friend across the sea. He founded a monastery and a church on the shore of Loch Lagan, and another in Fifeshire. St. Kenneth, as the Scotch called him, was noted for his eloquence and learning, and wrote a commentary on the four Gospels which was much valued in his day.

Drostan, one of the most beloved of the first companions of Columba, was chosen to govern a monastery founded on the east coast in the present district of Buchan. When he realized that the breadth of Scotland would henceforward separate him from the brethren whom he loved, and the father of his soul, he wept so bitterly that Columba declared that the new foundation should be called the "place of tears," and Déar (Deer) it remains to this day, to prove to us that the religious life has not the effect, as some people suppose, of hardening the hearts and freezing the affections of those who embrace it, but asks only that love go hand in hand with sacrifice in order that it may be conformed to the love of Christ.

Chapter VIII

THE CONVENTION OF DRUM-CEATT

COLUMBA had been eleven years at Iona when Conal, the King of the Scottish Dalriada, died. He was succeeded by Aidan, his cousin, whose love and veneration for Columbcille led him to choose him for his "soul's friend," and to beg him to come himself to place the crown upon his head and to pray that the grace of God might be with him in his governing. Columba assented to his request, and so it came to pass that the solemn rite of the consecration of a king was performed for the first time in the British Isles.

Aidan was crowned on the famous "Stone of Destiny" which was afterwards removed to Scone and was used as the coronation chair for the Kings of Scotland, until Edward I, "the Hammer of the Scots," carried it away and set it up in Westminster Abbey. Perhaps it was as well for the peace of mind of the ruthless oppressor that he could not look into the future, and see how the royal line of Scotland would in course of time follow the Stone of Destiny, and, crowned once more upon it, rule over the United Kingdom.

For Aidan was the ancestor of Macbeth and Malcolm Canmore, and through
the female line, of the Bruces and the Stuarts, while many of the old
Highland families, such as the Mackenzies, MacKinnons, Mackintoshes,
Macgregors, Macleans and Macnabs, count their descent from the
Dalriadan kinsmen of Columba.

The little kingdom had become powerful, and the yearly tribute to Ireland was galling to the pride of the Scots. They would fain have cast off the Irish yoke, and were quite ready to fight for their independence, but Columba bade them have patience, and all would be well. Diarmaid, his old enemy, had died a violent death, and Aedh MacAinmire, who was of Columba's own branch of the Hy-Nialls, now sat on the throne of Ireland: the time seemed ripe for the Saint to use his influence on behalf of Dalriada.

A large assembly or convention was about to be held at Drum-ceatt near Derry, to decide several important questions, some of which interested Columba nearly. It was a fitting moment, he thought, to obtain what they desired; and taking the King of Dalriada with him he set sail for Ireland.

The chief question which the Irish parliament had met to discuss, was the abolition or the banishment of the Bards. This ancient order of national poets dated from the earliest times, and in olden days had shared the power of the Druids. They were the guardians of the poetry, the history and the music of Ireland, and were held in such honour that the first place at table, after that reserved for the King, was theirs by right. A chief poet was entitled to a retinue of thirty men, and the Bards of a lower grade to fifteen. They had been loaded with honours by those of the princes and kings of Ireland who desired to have their brave deeds in battle handed down to their children or held up to the admiration of their rivals in the songs of the country.

Many abuses had arisen from such an exercise of power. The Bards in course of time had become thoroughly unpopular, and had only themselves to blame for the change of feeling towards them, for even their best friends could not defend their conduct. People had grown weary of an insolence that refused to sing the praises of the heroes and warriors of Erin unless at a price that few could afford to pay, and the Bards threatened to hold up those who displeased them to the contempt and ridicule of the nation.

The King went so far as to drive them from his palace, but so secure were they of their own power that they had the boldness to come back, and to demand of him the royal brooch that he wore upon his breast, the very token of his kingship. Beside himself with anger, the King announced his intention of doing away completely with the order of the Bards at the great Convention which was about to be held at Drum-ceatt, and their enemies, who were not few, resolved to see the threat carried out.

The Bards realized at last that they had gone too far, they could scarcely find a friend to speak for them, the situation was wellnigh hopeless. In their distress they thought of Columba, who had always befriended their order, and sent him a piteous message that their ruin was certain unless he would use his influence in their favour.

The Convention was largely attended. The two kings presided, and the presence of Columba, in company with many other abbots and bishops, gave dignity and order to the councils. The first question raised was that of the supremacy of Ireland over the Scots of Dalriada. Columba was asked to give his opinion, but fearful of being unduly influenced by his affection for Aidan, he asked his friend St. Colman to plead the cause of liberty. It was decided that Dalriada should cease to pay tribute and become an independent kingdom, on the condition that she promised a perpetual alliance with Ireland. The great question of the Bards came next, and on this subject the King himself was the first to speak. Their insolence, their idleness, and their greed, he said, had made them odious in the eyes of the whole nation. He therefore appealed to the assembly to banish them and to do away with all their privileges.

Not a voice was raised in their defence, and in another moment their fate would have been decided, when Columba rose to speak. The whole assembly did him reverence, and his clear voice rang out with all its old charm over the hearts of his countrymen.

It was true, he said, that the Bards had greatly abused their power; let therefore the abuses be corrected, let their power be diminished, let the guilty be punished. But if the great Bardic order were abolished, who would be left to make the records of the nation, to sing the noble deeds of its heroes or to lament the death of the brave? Where would be the glory of Erin? Why should the good grain be torn up with the tares? The poetry of Ireland, which was dear to her as her life, would perish for ever, were the order of poets to be destroyed.

The eloquent pleading of Columba carried all before it. It was decreed that the order should be reformed and that regular schools should be founded for the study of the literature of the nation, where the young poets might be brought up to devote their lives to their art, and to avoid the bad habits that had made the order so unpopular with the people. The Bards, who were themselves present at the assembly under the leadership of their chief, Dallan Forgaill, showed their gratitude to Columba by composing a poem in his praise. They wisely allowed themselves to be guided by his advice in their plans for reform, and in the establishment of the schools to which Ireland owes the preservation of the old chronicles and of the ancient literature in which she is so rich. They justified the plea of their protector and became faithful auxiliaries of the clergy, singing in the times of persecution the glory of the heroes and the Saints of Erin, and the beauty of the ancient faith.

When the assembly broke up, Columba paid a visit to Aedh in his royal palace, when he sought and obtained the freedom of Scandlan Mor, son of the King of Ossory, whom the High King of Ireland had unjustly detained in prison. The eldest son of Aedh was perhaps a little uneasy at the prospect of the visit, for he had received a severe reproof from the Saint for holding the monks of Iona up to ridicule; but Domnal, his younger brother, attached himself to Columbcille with a boy's enthusiastic admiration for all that is great and noble. Columba was delighted with the manly young prince, and prophesied that his reign would be a long and happy one, on condition that he "received the Holy Communion every week, and tried to keep his promises." He would also, he said, "die on his own feather-bed," a rare enough thing in the days when a King of Ireland was pretty sure to fall on the field of battle or to perish by the hand of an assassin.

Aedh himself had reason to be uneasy about the state of his soul, and asked Columba if any of the princes who had died during his reign were in heaven. He was told that three only had escaped the pains of purgatory and had entered into everlasting bliss.

"And I," asked the King, "shall I save my soul?"

"Not unless you repent heartily of all your sins and lead a better life," replied Columba; and Aedh resolved to take his advice.

To all the princes of Ireland, especially to those who were of his own blood, Columbcille preached compassion and mercy towards their enemies, the forgiveness of injuries, and the recall of exiles. Many of the latter had passed by Iona as they went to seek shelter in a strange land, and his heart had grieved with them in their sorrow.

He resolved also to visit his religious foundations in Ireland before he returned to the country of his adoption, and we can imagine the joy of the monks of Derry and Durrow who had never thought to look upon their beloved father's face again. The people came out in crowds to welcome him and carried a canopy of green branches over his head. Adamnan tells us of the miracles worked by the Saint on his journey, and how the labourers would leave their work as he passed and go before him singing hymns of joy.

As he was about to enter one of the monasteries, a poor little boy, who was looked upon by everybody as an idiot on account of his stammering tongue and vacant eye, crept through the crowd and took hold of the border of Columba's cloak. The Saint turned round, and taking the child in his arms embraced him tenderly.

"Show me your tongue," he said to the little boy, who was trembling with fear; and then, making the sign of the Cross over him, he turned to the bystanders, who were vexed that he should pay so much attention to an idiot.

"This child whom you despise so much," he said, "will grow daily in wisdom and virtue; God will give to him eloquence and power; and when he has grown to man's estate he will be counted amongst the great ones of his country."

The Saint's prophecy came true. The little idiot boy grew into the great St. Ernan, venerated both in Ireland and Scotland; and it was he himself who told the story to the abbot Adamnan who wrote the great life of Columbcille.

Chapter IX

FOR CHRIST AND HIS LOVE

THE visitation of the Irish monasteries completed, Columba returned to Iona. But it was no longer as an exile that he left the shores of Erin. This time it was to "Hy of his love, and Hy of his heart" that he was bound—to the country that had become dear to him as the land of his adoption and of his mission; where he had suffered and striven for his Master's sake, and where his work had been blessed beyond all that he had hoped or dreamed.

It is especially during the last few years of Columba's life on earth that we can see how the natural fire and arrogance of his nature had been gradually transformed into the gentleness and charity of Christ. It was not without many a struggle that the transformation took place; but Columbcille was a man of great heart and of determined will; what he set himself to do was sure to be done. Now he had set himself—with God's grace—to self-conquest, and the work, though not to be completed in a day nor yet in a year, was at last by dint of prayer and patience gloriously achieved. The gentleness of a naturally strong and fiery temperament won—so to speak—at the sword's point, is always an extraordinary force in the world, and we find the power of Columba over his fellow-men and his influence with them for good increasing every year.

St. Fintan, one of the Saint's first companions in Iona, was asked once towards the end of Columba's life to describe him to one who had heard much of his holiness, but who did not know him.

"He is a king amongst kings," answered Fintan, "a sage amongst wise men, a monk amongst monks. He is poor with God's poor; a mourner with those who weep, and joyful with those who rejoice. Yet amidst all the gifts of nature and of grace that have been so liberally showered on him by God, the true humility of Christ is as royally rooted in his heart as if it were its natural home."

He was the father, the brother and the friend of all who were in want or distress; the dauntless champion of the oppressed and of the weak, the avenger of all who suffered wrong. His prayers and blessing were sought by all the navigators of the stormy seas of the Hebrides as a defence against the dangers of the deep; while during his journeys on the mainland the people would bring out their sick and lay them in his path, that they might touch the hem of his cloak or receive his benediction as he passed. Their simple faith was not in vain: many were the miraculous cures wrought by the Saint, whose prayers were as powerful with God as those of St. Peter and St. John, and with whom he might have said "silver and gold I have none, but what I have I give thee."

  He would visit rich and poor alike, and it was often in the houses of the latter that he met with the truest hospitality. He would find out with gentle tact what were the means of his humble hosts, and plan ways of increasing their little store. Once when he was passing through Lochaber on his way to visit King Bruidh in his royal palace, he was offered a lodging in the house of a poor peasant and kindly entertained with the best that the poverty of the house could furnish. In the morning when the little Highland cows of his host were being driven out to pasture, Columbcille blessed them, and foretold that they would increase until in course of time they would number five hundred, and that the blessing of a grateful traveller would rest upon the man and his family.

  Columba took an observant interest in all the things of nature, and was often able to advise the peasants how to improve the simple methods of farming, hunting, and fishing on which their daily food depended. On one occasion he profited by the hospitality shown to him by a rich Highland chief to put an end to a deadly feud which in true Highland fashion had existed for many years between his host and one of his neighbours. The enemies were reconciled, and both became fast friends of the peacemaker.

  Tender-hearted as Columba was to all who were in sorrow and distress, to none did his ready sympathy extend more fully than to those who were exiles from their native land, for he remembered the early days of his own sojourn in Iona. One of his special friends was a Pictish chief of noble birth who had received him on the occasion of his first missionary journey to Caledonia and treated him with generous hospitality. Some time after he fell into disgrace and was banished from the country. Columba appealed in his favour to Feradagh, the chief of the island of Islay, whom he begged to give shelter and protection to the exile, while he tried what his influence could do with the Pictish king to obtain his friend's recall. Feradagh, after promising hospitality to the fugitive, murdered him treacherously for the sake of his possessions. The news was brought to Columbcille, who cried out in indignation that the punishment of God would overtake the traitor before he had tasted of the flesh of the boars that he was fattening for his table.

Feradagh laughed at the threat but was not a little uneasy, for he had heard of the strange way in which Columba's prophecies were wont to come true. He had a boar killed without loss of time and roasted, in order to reassure himself that this time at least the Saint had been wrong. As he sat down to table, he fell down from his seat and died, to the fear and consternation of his followers.

A certain chief named Donnell, who with his sons and followers feared neither God nor man, was the terror of all the neighbouring country. Although he could claim kinship with the King of Dalriada, Columba excommunicated him for his deeds of violence, and he and his family vowed vengeance on the Saint. Taking advantage of a journey that Columba was making to a neighbouring island with only one or two companions, one of the sons of Donnell resolved to murder him as he slept. But one of Columbcille's companions, a monk named Finn Lugh, was beset that night with an unaccountable fear for the safety of his holy abbot, and begged him to lend him his cowl, in which he wrapped himself and lay down to sleep. In the dead of night the assassin crept upon the little band of travellers, and, seeking out the monk who wore the abbot's cowl, stabbed him, and fled to a place of safety. But the garment of the Saint protected the man who was ready to give his life for his master, and Finn Lugh escaped without a wound.

Another lawless member of the same family fell upon and robbed a man who lived upon the rocky peninsula of Ardnamurchan, and had constantly shown hospitality to Columba on his journeys. The blessing of the Saint had brought him good fortune, and his little patrimony had increased year by year. The people, in honour of the affection shown him by the holy abbot, called him "Columbain" or "the friend of Columba." As the robber was returning, laden with the spoils of the poor man, to the boat that was awaiting him at the water's edge, he met Columba himself, whom he had supposed to be safely distant at Iona. The Saint reproved him sternly for his crimes, and bade him restore the goods that he had stolen. The robber chief maintained a grim silence until he was safely in his boat and well out from the shore. Then he stood up, and bursting into a storm of insults and evil words, shouted defiance and derision at Columbcille as long as his voice could be heard. The oppression of the helpless never failed to rouse Columba's wrath. He strode out into the water after the retreating boat, and, raising his arms to heaven, prayed that justice might be done on the robber. Then returning quietly to his companions he said to them, "That wicked man who despises Christ in His poor will return no more to these shores. The cup of his iniquity is full." Shortly afterwards a storm arose, and the boat with all that were in it sank like a stone between Mull and Colonsay.

But it was not only to the poor and the oppressed that Columba's charity was shown. We find him at the Court of King Aidan, holding his young son Hector "the Blond" in his arms and praying that his life might be as fair as his features. To the nobles who kept the laws of God he was as devoted a friend as he was a steadfast opponent of those who outraged them. To the penitent he was full of mercy and hope, and many sinners were persuaded by his eloquence and power to forsake their evil ways.

But nowhere was his charity more clearly shown than with his own community at Iona. He foresaw the needs of all, and watched over his spiritual sons with a fatherly love and care. During one of the last summers of his life when the monks were coming back in the evening after a day of harvesting, they stopped short at a little distance from the monastery to enjoy the sense of peace and consolation that seemed to come to meet them as they approached their home.

"How is it," asked one of the younger brethren, "that at this spot every night when we return from our daily labours, our hearts rejoice, our burdens grow light, and the very perfume of heaven seems borne to us on the breeze?"

"I will tell you," said Baithen, the beloved friend and successor of Columba. "Our saintly abbot, whose heart is with us in our work, is praying for us and longing for our safe return. His heart is heavy with our weariness, and, having no longer the strength to come in the body to meet us and help us with our burdens, he sends forth the blessing and the prayer of his soul to refresh and console us on our way."

Not only his fellow-men but all the creatures of God were dear to Columba for their Creator's sake. One day he bade a certain monk at Iona go down to the seashore and watch.

"For," said the Saint, "ere the night falls a weary guest will arrive to us from Ireland, faint and ready to die. Succour her and tend her carefully for three days, and when she is rested and refreshed let her go, that she may return once more to her native land." The guest was a poor storm-driven crane which fell on the shore exhausted at the brother's feet. He bore it tenderly to the monastery and cared for it as his master had bidden. In the evening Columba met the monk and blessed him for his compassion to the weary stranger; and, as he had foretold, on the third day, strengthened and refreshed the bird took its flight back to Erin.

Chapter X

THE GIFT OF VISION

WE have already seen how it was often given to St. Columba to know of events that were happening far away from the place where he might be, and how by his gift of prophecy he could sometimes foretell what would come to pass in the future. As he grew older it seemed to those who knew him intimately that these flashes of supernatural insight became more frequent, and that the things of the next world were growing daily more familiar to him as the time of his earthly pilgrimage drew to an end. Many instances of this have been recorded by his biographers.

One morning at Iona when the Mass was about to be celebrated, Columba sent word to the priest whose turn it was to offer the Holy Sacrifice that day, to do it in honour of the glorious birthday of St. Brendan. The monk could not understand his abbot's behest as no word had reached Iona of the holy Brendan's death. Columba then told him that during the night he had seen in a vision the soul of Brendan ascending to heaven surrounded by a great company of rejoicing angels; he knew therefore that he had entered into his rest.

On another occasion he ordered that the Mass for the feast of a bishop should be sung. Now there was no feast marked in the calendar for that day, and the monks asked their holy abbot to tell them the name of the bishop in whose honour the Holy Mysteries were to be celebrated.

"Last night," he replied, "I saw the soul of Columban, the Bishop of Leinster, in heaven, surrounded with the glory of the blessed; it is in his honour that we must offer the Holy Sacrifice to-day."

Columba had a deep love and reverence for all honest labour done for God. One night he told his monks that he had just seen entering into heaven the soul of a blacksmith whom he had known long ago in Ireland.

"He has bought eternal life," he said, "with the labours of the earthly. He was charitable and gave of his poverty to the poor, therefore the Lord of the Poor has rewarded him."

In the course of his travels in the Highlands he met one day in a lonely gorge a countryman in great distress. He was returning from a journey, and had heard that during his absence from home, a band of Saxon marauders had laid waste his little farm and burnt his house to the ground. He was in an anguish of fear lest his wife and children should have perished. Columba comforted him with kind words.

"Go in peace, my good man," he said, "your cattle and all your possessions have, it is true, been carried off by the robbers; but God has been merciful. Your dear little family is safe; go, for your loved ones are waiting for you, and comfort their sorrowing hearts."

Again, a year after the attempt had been made to murder Columba and the monk Finn Lugh had saved his life, the Saint asked his companion if he remembered the occurrence.

"It is just a year ago to-day," he said, "since Donnell tried to murder me, and our dear Finn Lugh would have given his life for mine. At this very moment the would-be murderer has been struck down by an enemy in punishment for his evil deeds."

One of the Saxon converts of the Saint had joined the community at Iona, and had been given charge of the bakehouse. Columba would often go to encourage him in his labours and to speak to him of the things of God. One day the Saxon saw him suddenly raise his eyes to heaven and join his hands in prayer. "Happy, happy woman," he cried, "to whom it is given to enter into the heavenly kingdom, carried by the hands of the angels."

A year afterwards when speaking to the same man, he said to him, "Do you remember the woman whose soul I saw a year ago ascending into heaven? I see her now coming to fetch the soul of her husband who is just dead. She is fighting with her prayers for that beloved soul against the powers of evil, and the angels are praying with her. See! she conquers, she bears him off, for he has led a good and upright life, and the two who loved each other so dearly on this earth are united for ever in the joy and glory of heaven."

Columbcille seems indeed to have had some such intimation from God of the death of the greater number of his friends; a vision of the glory of that celestial country into which he was himself soon to enter, and after which he sighed with such ardent longing. If the angels had been with him in his youth, much more did they surround him in his later years.

Many stories are told of his celestial visions as he prayed in the forests of Skye, dear to him for their loneliness and silence. One dy, when he was at Iona he went out, giving orders that no one was to follow him. He was going to pray, he said, on a little hill to the west of Iona, which was one of his favourite retreats. One young brother, more curious than the rest, had heard strange tales about the holy abbot, and followed him carefully from afar to see what was going to happen. When he had come within a short distance of the place of prayer, he saw the Saint standing with arms raised to heaven, surrounded by a troop of white-robed angels. The young monk, trembling lest he should be discovered, made his way back to the monastery as quickly as he could.

When Columba rose during the night as was his habit to kneel in prayer on the cold floor of his cell, his heavenly visitors would throng around him, mingling their praise with his. It was not surprising that the things of heaven should be so near to one who cared so little for the things of earth. He would go out on a winter's night, says his biographer, and stand in the waters of an icy stream during the time it took him to recite the Psalter, that he might obtain grace by his sufferings for the souls of the obstinate sinners who refused to amend their lives. One day when he was praying in a lonely spot, a poor woman came in sight gathering wild herbs and nettles. Columba spoke to her and asked her what she was doing.

"I am gathering herbs for food," she replied, "for I have but one cow and it gives no milk; the poor must live as they can." Columba reproached himself bitterly that this poor woman should fare worse than he did. "We seek to win heaven," he cried, "by our austerities, and this poor woman, who is under no such obligation, outdoes us." Henceforward he declared he would make his meal of the wild herbs and nettles that he had seen her gathering, and gave strict orders that nothing else should be served to him. He even reproved Baithen, whom he so dearly loved, with unwonted severity, because, unable to bear the sight of his abbot's wretched fare, he had put a little piece of butter into the pot in which it was being cooked.

The heavenly light that the holy Brendan had seen surrounding Columba on that memorable day at Teilte was now frequently beheld by his companions. At night it could be seen shining through the chinks in the rough door of his little cell when all was in darkness, and the silence of the night was only broken by the voice of the holy abbot praying and singing the praises of God.

One winter's night, one of the younger brethren had remained in the church to pray after all had gone to rest. At midnight the door opened softly and Columba entered. A glory of golden light came with him, illuminating the church from wall to wall and from floor to roof. The little chapel where the brother knelt was flooded with the strange radiance and his soul was filled with a heavenly consolation. Columba knelt for many hours in prayer, and still the heavenly light shone round him as he prayed; while the brother watched him awestruck, scarcely daring to move for fear of being heard. The next day he was sent for by the abbot, who blessed him and gently bade him say nothing of what he had seen during the night.

Two of his religious, Baithen the beloved, and Diarmaid his faithful attendant, who were often in his cell to help him with his work and to carry out his instructions, noticed one day a sudden ray of joy shining from their master's eyes. A moment later the joyful expression gave place to one of intense sadness, and they begged Columba to reveal to them what it was that caused him grief.

"My children," said the Saint, "it is twenty years to-day since I first set foot in Caledonia. Earnestly I have been beseeching our Heavenly Father to bring my days of exile to an end, and to receive me into the heavenly country after which our hearts must ever yearn. It seemed to me that God had heard my prayer, and that I already saw the holy angels coming to bear my soul to its eternal Home, when suddenly they faded from my sight, and I saw them no more. It has been revealed to me that by reason of the prayers of those who love me on earth, the time of my sojourning has been prolonged. Therefore am I sad, beloved of my heart, because four long years must elapse before those heavenly messengers return. Then they will come once more and I shall depart with them to rejoice for ever in the presence of my God."

Chapter XI

THE LIGHT ETERNAL

IT was towards the end of May, when the late northern springtime was casting its veil of beauty over the rugged islands of the Hebrides, that Columbcille knew that the time of his departure was at hand. He bade his faithful attendant Diarmaid harness the oxen into the rude wooden cart of the monastery, and taking his seat in it set out for the fields that lay to the west of the island where all the monks were working. At the sight of the abbot in his humble chariot they left their work and crowded round him, and the old man addressed them tenderly with touching words of affection.

"A month ago," he said, "I had a great desire to depart from this earth, that I might keep the happy festival of Easter in heaven; but, unwilling to cast a gloom over your joy at that glad time, I was content to remain with you a little longer. But now the time of my earthly pilgrimage draws near its end." At these words the monks broke into bitter weeping, for the thought of losing their beloved father was more than they could bear, and Columba tried to comfort them. Then standing erect in the waggon he raised his hands and blessed the island, the monastery and all its inhabitants.

A few days later, leaning on Diarmaid's arm, he went to the barn and rejoiced to see the great heaps of corn laid up for the winter. "It is a comfort to me to know," he said, "that when I am no longer there my children will not go hungry. For this year at least there is plentiful provision."

"Why do you break our hearts, dear Father, in this sweet season of the year," said Diarmaid, "by speaking so often of your departure from us? God will surely suffer us to keep you with us yet awhile."

"I will tell you a secret, Diarmaid," replied the old man; "but first you must promise to keep it faithfully till I am dead."

And when Diarmaid had promised, kneeling at the abbot's feet, "To-morrow, Sunday, is the day of rest," he said, "but before the dawning of that day, I shall have entered into the rest which is eternal. To-night at midnight I shall depart from this world; it has been revealed to me by our Lord Jesus Christ Himself."

Then Diarmaid could no longer control his grief and wept aloud while the Saint did his best to comfort him, speaking words of hope and consolation. On their way home from the barn to the monastery Columba grew weary, and sat down to rest by the wayside, at a spot where there is now a great stone cross. As he sat there waiting until he should have strength to continue his journey, the old white horse that used to carry the milk pails from the farm to the monastery came up and laid its head upon the Saint's shoulder, looking at him as if he knew that it was for the last time, with eyes so full of dumb grief that they seemed to be shedding tears. Diarmaid would have driven him away, but Columba checked him.

"Let him be," he said; "he is wiser than you, Diarmaid, for he knows by instinct that I shall never pass by this way again. The old horse loves me, let him grieve for his friend."

Then the faithful animal nestled his head closer against the shoulder of the old man, who caressed him gently and gave him his blessing. "It is God," he said, "who has made known to this poor beast that he will see me no more." When continuing their journey they had reached the little hill that overlooked the monastery, Columba raised his hands in blessing over his beloved island home.

"This place will be famous in the days to come," he said, "and saints and kings will come from other lands to do it honour."

When he reached his cell he sat down to write the copy of the Psalter on which he was engaged, for the old man's hand had not lost its skill. He wrote until the church bell rang for the first vespers of the Sunday; then, having reached the verse in the thirty-third Psalm where it is written "They that seek the Lord shall not be deprived of any good," he laid down the pen.

"Let Baithen write the rest," he said.

Baithen was the cousin of Columba, and one of the monks who had come with him from Derry. He had been his pupil, and was scarcely less skilful with the pen than his master. Holy, charitable, and beloved by all, he was chosen to succeed Columbcille as abbot of Iona. When he took up the pen that the Saint had laid down to go on with the work of transcription, the words that came next were, "Come ye children, hearken unto me, and I will teach you the fear of the Lord," with which words he began his ministry as abbot.

When Vespers were over, Columba went back to his cell and sitting down upon his bed—the naked rock with a stone for a pillow that was still the only couch on which this monk of seventy-seven would rest his aged limbs—he bade Diarmaid listen while he gave him his last instructions for the brethren.

"My last words to you are these," said he. "Cherish true and unfeigned charity ever amongst yourselves, and God will never leave you in need, but will give you all that is necessary for your welfare in this world, and His glory in that which is to come."

After these words he was silent, and seemed to be lost in the contemplation of the glory of which he had spoken, and Diarmaid forbore to interrupt his prayer. When the bell rang for matins shortly before midnight, Columba arose, and went swiftly to the church. Diarmaid followed more slowly, and as he approached the door, the whole church seemed to him to be lit up with a strangely radiant light which vanished as he entered. "Where are you, Father?" he whispered, struck with a sudden fear, as he groped his way through the building. There was no answer. He made his way through the darkness as best he could to the altar.

There in his accustomed place of prayer was the holy abbot, but stretched apparently lifeless on the ground. Diarmaid raised him in his arms, and sitting down beside him laid the beloved head upon his shoulder. Presently the brethren came in with lights, and broke into bitter lamentation at the scene before them. Columba lay on the altar steps leaning on Diarmaid's breast, his eyes raised to heaven, and his face shining with a wondrous joy as if he already saw its gates opening before him. Diarmaid then raised his master's right hand, and for the last time the holy abbot blessed his little flock who knelt weeping round him, while his eyes spoke the words that his voice was too weak to utter. Then with one last upward look his head sank gently back on Diarmaid's shoulder and he gave up his pure soul to God. They could scarcely believe that he was dead, for his face was still so bright with joy that he looked like one who rested in a happy and peaceful sleep. The matins for that Sunday were sung with bursting hearts, for the strong clear voice that had always been foremost in the holy chant was silent for ever ....

During that night a vision came to a holy old man in one of the monasteries of Ireland. He saw the island of Iona all aflame with a glorious light and a multitude of angels descending from the skies. He heard them singing as they bore the blessed soul of Columbcille back with them into heaven, and the celestial melody filled his heart with joy.

At the same hour a boy named Ernene who was fishing by night in the River Finn in Donegal saw the whole sky suddenly break into light. In the east where Iona lay, there rose a great pillar of fire, so that for one moment the night was as bright as the noonday when the sun is shining. Then it vanished into the heavens and all was dark again.

It might have been expected that the little island would be crowded with men thronging from all directions to the funeral of Columbcille, but it was not so. While the Saint was yet alive one of the monks had said to him that Iona would be scarcely large enough to hold the numbers that would come to pay him the last honours.

"No, my son," replied Columba, "no one will be there but those of our own household;" and so it came to pass.

On the night of the Saint's death a violent storm arose, and continued until the burial was over; the sea was so wild that no boat could put out from the mainland or the surrounding islands. The simple rites were performed in the presence of the monks of Iona alone, to the sound of the wailing of the wind and the moaning of the sea. Was it the last revenge of the evil one, they asked themselves, on the Saint who had torn a nation from his grasp?

But Columbcille had passed
   To where beyond these voices there is peace.

Lightning Source UK Ltd.
Milton Keynes UK
UKHW021826110119
335424UK00028B/986/P

9 781544 643809

Lightning Source UK Ltd.
Milton Keynes UK
UKHW021826110119
335424UK00028B/986/P